S0-AKM-767

PETUNIA
the Silly Goose
Stories

PETUNIA
the Silly Goose
Stories

Written and illustrated by
ROGER DUVOISIN

ALFRED A. KNOPF · NEW YORK

THIS IS A BORZOI BOOK PUBLISHED BY ALFRED A. KNOPF, INC.

Copyright © 1987 by Louise A. Duvoisin.
All rights reserved under International and Pan-American
Copyright Conventions. Published in the United States by Alfred A.
Knopf, Inc., New York, and simultaneously in Canada by Random
House of Canada Limited, Toronto. Distributed by Random House,
Inc., New York. All the works contained in this book were originally
published 1950–1975. *Petunia:* Copyright 1950 by Alfred A. Knopf,
Inc. Copyright renewed 1977 by Roger Duvoisin. *Petunia's
Christmas:* Copyright 1952 by Alfred A. Knopf, Inc. Copyright
renewed 1980 by Roger Duvoisin. *Petunia's Treasure:* Copyright ©
1975 by Roger Duvoisin. *Petunia Takes a Trip:* Copyright 1953 by
Alfred A. Knopf, Inc. Copyright renewed 1981 by Louise A.
Duvoisin. *Petunia, Beware!* Copyright © 1958 by Roger Duvoisin.
Copyright renewed 1986 by Louise A. Duvoisin.

Book design by Mina Greenstein
Additional color separations by Bruce McGowan
Manufactured in the United States of America
2   4   6   8   10   9   7   5   3   1

Library of Congress Cataloging-in-Publication Data
Duvoisin, Roger, 1900–1980. Petunia the silly goose stories.
Contents: 1. Petunia—2. Petunia's Christmas—3. Petunia's
treasure—[etc.] 1. Children's stories, American.
[1. Geese—Fiction]
I. Title. PZ7.D957Pf 1987 [Fic] 86-2783
ISBN: 0-394-88292-X (trade); 0-394-98292-4 (lib. bdg.)

Contents

PETUNIA

In the meadow, early one morning, Petunia, the silly goose, went strolling. She ate a bug here, clipped off a clover leaf there, and she picked at the dewdrops on the goldenrod leaves.

3

Then, suddenly, she saw something she had never seen before in the meadow. What was it?

4

Petunia stole closer and closer
and sniffed at it from all sides.

"By Goosey Gander," she said, "it does not
smell like food for a goose. But I believe I
have seen such a thing before. . . .

"Yes, I have seen one under Bill's arm when he came out of school. It's a Book. That's it. A BOOK!

"Come to think of it, just the other day I heard Mr. Pumpkin telling Bill that Books are very precious. 'He who owns Books and loves them is wise.' That is what he said.

6

"He who owns Books and loves them is wise," repeated Petunia to herself. And she thought as hard and as long as she could. "Well, then," she said at last, "if I take this Book with me, and love it, I will be wise too. And no one will call me a silly goose ever again."

So Petunia picked up the Book, and off she went with it.

She slept with it . . .   she swam with it.

And, knowing that she was so wise, Petunia also became proud,

and prouder   and prouder. . .   so proud

that her neck stretched out several notches.

It was King, the rooster, who first noticed the change in
Petunia. He said, "Maybe Petunia is not so silly after all. She has
a Book. And she looks so wise that she must be so."

And the other animals began to believe in Petunia's wisdom
too. They asked her for advice and opinions, and Petunia was
glad to help—even when she was not asked.

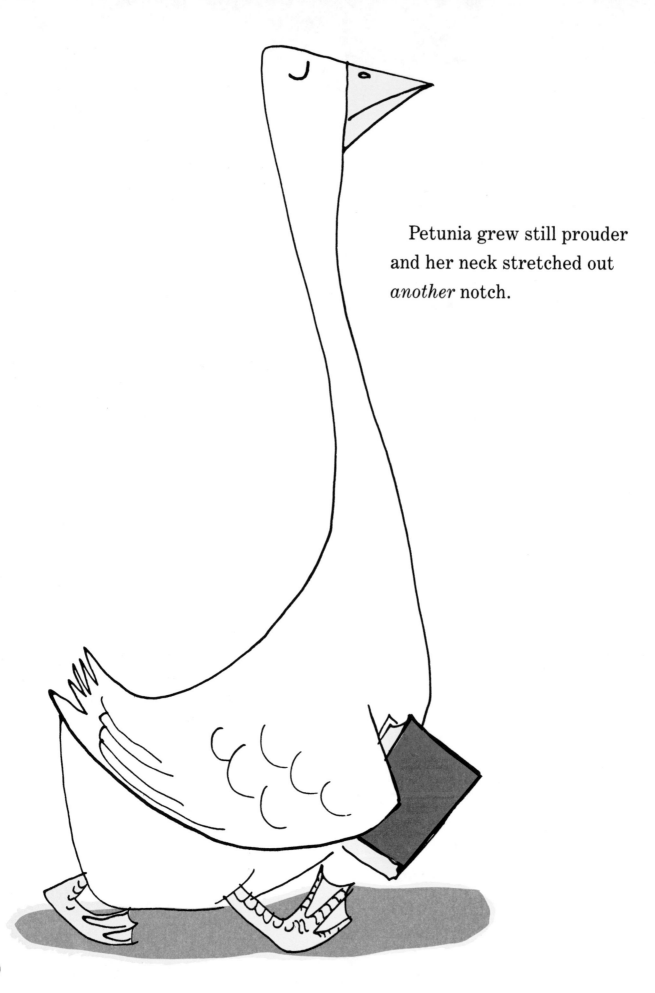

Petunia grew still prouder
and her neck stretched out
another notch.

One day Petunia heard Clover, the cow, say to King, the
rooster, "I wonder what makes your comb so red, King—as red
as the barn."

"It's my blood," said King. "It's the color of my blood."

"Nonsense," said Clover. "I have blood too. But I'm not a red
cow. Your comb has been dipped in red barn-paint, that's what
makes it so red."

"You are both silly, of course," said Petunia. "King, your comb
was stuck on by the farmer so he can tell you from the hens and
know who lays eggs and who doesn't. Plastic comb, I'd say."

And so King never again shook his proud comb in song for fear
it might fall off.

Poor sad rooster.

But Petunia had other things to do.

At the chicken coop, Ida, the hen, was cackling excitedly
among her chicks. "Oh, Petunia," she said, "my chicks and I have
been for a walk in the woods, and I think I've lost some of them.
The farmer says I had nine but I can't count so very well.
Please, wise Petunia, count my chicks to see if they're all here."

"Glad to help," said Petunia. "Hm. Let's see. Three chicks at the fountain. Three at the feeder. Three about your legs. Now—three times three? That makes six . . ."

"Six?" asked Ida. "Six! Is that less than nine?"

"That's *more* than nine, not less," said Petunia. "*Lots* more, my dear!"

"*More than nine?* Good gracious! As if I hadn't enough worries with my own nine chicks. And where do those other chicks come from? Oh, dear, I'll never be happy again."

Poor worried Ida.

But Petunia had other things to do.

In the meadow she discovered part of Noisy, the dog, sticking out of a hole in the ground.

"Help! Help!" cried Noisy. "I stuck my head in this rabbit hole, and now it won't come out. Help!"

"Glad to help," said Petunia. "It's a good thing I know what hunters do to get stubborn animals out of holes in the ground. They *smoke* them out. Wait until I fetch some sticks and some matches."

And so, wise Petunia built a fire in the other end of the hole
and fanned it well with the Book.

Her trick worked nicely. Noisy, choking with smoke, jerked his
his head out of the hole and ran off howling with pain. His nose
was singed with the fire, and his ears were cut and bruised.

Poor moaning dog.

But Petunia had other things to do.

Beside the hedgerow she met Straw, the horse, who was in pain from a toothache.

"Petunia," groaned Straw, "I'm dying. Surely, with your wisdom, you can stop this horrible pain."

"Glad to help," said Petunia. "Open your mouth. Why . . . you poor Straw . . . all these teeth! No wonder you have a toothache.

"Look at me. Do I have teeth? Of course not. So I have no toothache. I am going to stop that pain right now. I am going to pull *all* those teeth out. *All* of them. Let me get some pliers . . ."

But Straw would not wait for the pliers. He was so afraid to lose his teeth that he never talked of his toothache to another soul. He suffered in silence.

Poor forlorn horse.

But Petunia had other things to do.

Cotton, the kitten, went up the tree but could not come down. While he miaowed and miaowed, his friends called for Petunia.

"Glad to help," said Petunia. "I know just what to do. Since none of you is tall enough to reach Cotton, all of you will do it together. Donkey on top of Clover, Pig on top of Donkey, and so on up. Simple."

So Donkey climbed on top of Clover;

Pig on top of Donkey;

Goat on top of Pig;

Sheep on top of Goat;

Piggy on top of Sheep;

Turkey on top of Piggy;

Duck on top of Turkey;

Hen on top of Duck. . . .

Suddenly Clover cried out,

"Stop! My legs feel wobbly."

And she sat . . .

. . . and Donkey and the rest
fell into a heap, and
Cotton was so scared that
he fell on top of them.
They were all full of bumps.

  "Well," said Petunia, "Cotton
is *down*."

  So he was, poor bruised kitten.

But Petunia had other things to do. Getting prouder all the time, she felt her neck stretch further out.

She now wandered down the meadow, where she found some other friends gathered around a box.

"Ah, wise Petunia!" they shouted. "We found this box in the ditch beside the road. Maybe it's food, Petunia. Please tell us what the writing on it says."

"Glad to help," said Petunia. "Now, let's see . . . Why, CANDIES. That's what it says on that box. Yes, candies. You may eat them. Yes, of course."

No sooner had Petunia given the word than seven greedy
mouths tore up the box and grabbed the candies out of it,
and . . .

BOOM

What a sight the animals were!

Some were burned.

Some were bruised.

Straw still suffered in silence.

Noisy still moaned.

Ida still worried about her chicks.

King still brooded over his comb.

All the barnyard was in trouble, and all because of Petunia.

Petunia's pride and wisdom had exploded with the firecrackers.

Her neck had shrunk back to its old size and was all bandaged up. She was the most downhearted of all, for she saw now that she was not a bit wise.

But suddenly Petunia spied the Book. The firecrackers had blown it open so that the pages showed. She had never seen them before. Now she saw that there was something written inside the Book which she could not read. So she sat down and thought and thought and thought, until at last she sighed, "Now I understand. It was not enough to carry wisdom under my wing. I must put it in my mind and in my heart. And to do that I must learn to read."

Petunia was filled with joy. At once she began to work so that one day she could be truly wise. Then she would help make her friends happy.

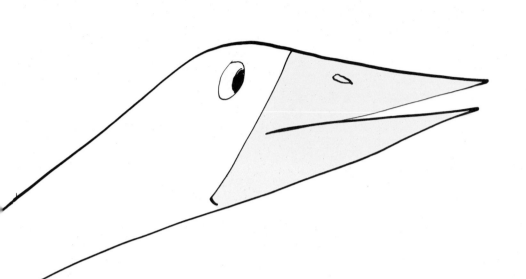

PETUNIA,
BEWARE!

Petunia never ate what she had in her own dish. Hoping for a better treat, she always ate from her friends' dishes.

She *never* touched the grass on her side of the fence, but *always* clipped what she could from the neighbor's meadow. Foolish Petunia never liked what was in her own yard. She wanted only what she didn't have.

"Ah," she sighed, looking through the fence at the grassy hills across the stream. "Think of the fine meals I am missing every day. How green is the grass on Windy Hill.

"Noisy," she said to the dog, "let's leave our yard and taste the wonderful green grass in the meadow beyond the fence."

"I never eat grass," yawned Noisy, "which shouldn't stop you from going alone. *BUT* beware of the wild animals!"

Foolish Petunia flicked her wing feathers and walked out into the wild, wide, greener world.

She plucked some grass from the neighbor's meadow.
BUT

The grass *wasn't* a bit greener.
It *wasn't* a bit tastier.
IT WAS THE SAME GRASS!

"Well," she said, "I'll walk on further."

"Good morning, Petunia," said the rabbit, popping out from under a stump. "Where are you going?"

"Good morning, Mr. Rabbit," said Petunia. "I am going to the next meadow to eat the greener, tastier grass under the old oak tree."

"Beware of the cruel weasel, Petunia. He poked his nose under my stump this very morning and gave me such a fright."

Petunia pulled a beakful of grass from under the old oak tree.
BUT

The grass *wasn't* a bit greener.
It *wasn't* a bit tastier.
IT WAS THE SAME GRASS!

"Well," she said, "let's walk further."

"Good morning, Petunia," said the woodchuck, peering out of
his hole. "Where are you going?"

"Good morning, Mr. Woodchuck. I am going to that meadow
beyond the dogwoods to eat the greener, tastier grass."

"Beware of the fox, Petunia. I smelled his tracks past the
stone fence this very dawn. The thief."

Petunia pulled a few blades of grass from the meadow beyond the dogwoods. *BUT*

The grass *wasn't* a bit greener.
It *wasn't* a bit tastier.
IT WAS THE SAME GRASS!

"Well," she said, "I'll just have to walk further."

"Good morning, Petunia," chattered the chipmunk, sitting up straight on a maple stump. "Where are you going?"

"Good morning, Mr. Chipmunk. I am going to that meadow at the edge of the brook to eat the greener, tastier grass."

"Beware of the fierce old raccoon, Petunia. He peeped into my hole this very morning, but my hole is too small for his claws."

When she reached the meadow at the edge of the brook,
Petunia could hardly believe that

The grass *wasn't* a bit greener.
It *wasn't* a bit tastier.
IT WAS THE SAME GRASS!

"Well," she said, "let's walk further."

"Good morning, Petunia," said the deer, browsing at the edge of the wood. "Where are you going?"

"Good morning, Mr. Deer. I am going to the meadow on top of Windy Hill to eat the greener, tastier grass."

"Beware of the bobcat, Petunia. It slunk past the deer-crossing early this morning."

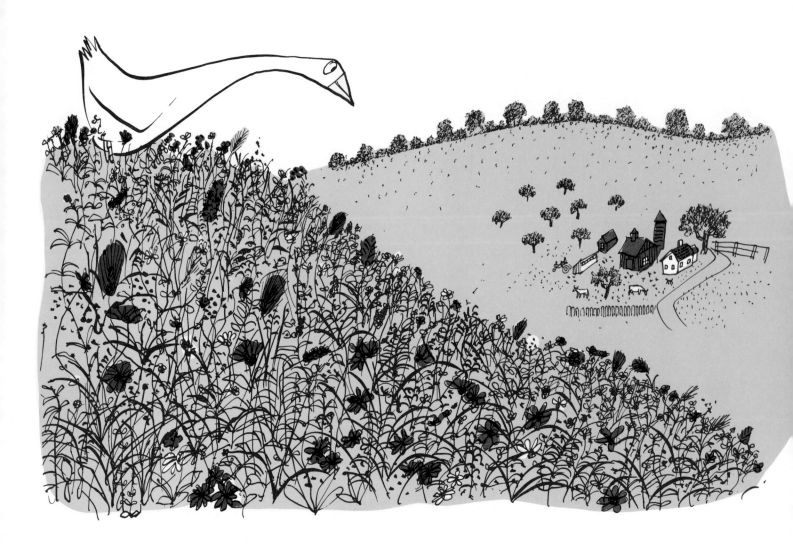

When Petunia reached the top of Windy Hill, she could hardly
believe it. *BUT*

The grass was not green.
It was not tasty.
IT WAS DRY GRASS.

"Well," she said, looking down the hill at her farm below, "how
VERY GREEN the grass looks in the meadow near the barn. I
never thought my own meadow looked so green and tasty. Well,
let's walk back."

"Why hurry, Petunia?" said a little voice behind her. "You are the loveliest, fattest goose I have ever seen. And I am so hungry."

IT WAS THE CRUEL WEASEL!

"Yes, do stay, Petunia," said a rasping voice behind a bush.
"Do not listen to the kind words of our friend. The weasel will
not touch one of your feathers while I am with you."

IT WAS THE FOX!

"Yes, don't leave quite yet, Petunia," said a silky voice from
the long grass. "Do not fear Weasel and Fox while I am here."

IT WAS THE FIERCE OLD RACCOON!

"Yes, do wait a while, Petunia," said a soft, purring voice from a clump of birches. "Weasel, Fox, and Raccoon will not harm you while I am protecting you."

IT WAS THE BOBCAT!

Petunia was so cold with fear that she could not move. She closed her eyes and thought of her farm in the lovely green valley.

The four greedy rascals leaped forward all together. They crashed into a hissing, yowling, clawing, biting jumble. The jumble looked like a four-headed dragon with sixteen legs and four tails. Petunia gathered all her strength and rushed down the hill, half running, half sliding (she was too heavy to fly well). She had reached the meadow at the edge of the brook when her enemies saw that she was gone.

They ran and tumbled down the hill after her. Over the brook,
past the dogwood trees, and through the meadow with the old
oak tree they ran.

But they were too LATE.

As Petunia, honking faintly, reached the neighbor's meadow,
Noisy the dog dashed out barking LOUDLY and put Weasel,
Fox, Raccoon, and Bobcat to flight.

After Petunia had thanked Noisy, she recovered enough to pull
a few blades of grass from her own meadow—*AND*—

IT WAS THE BEST GRASS
THAT SHE HAD
EVER TASTED.

PETUNIA'S TREASURE

Petunia loved to swim in the river at the end of the meadow where great rocks and fir trees rose high above the water. One day, as she dived deep into the cave under the rocks, she saw a big trunk with brass locks that shone in the dark.

"That's a treasure chest," thought Petunia. "I know a treasure chest as well as anyone else. Pirates hid it here hundreds of years ago. That's what they always did."

She swam up to the bank to sit and think.
"Finding a treasure makes one rich. That's well known. So I
must be rich. I am a rich and important person."

She walked back to the Pumpkin farmyard with head high and pride in her eyes.

"What ails you, Petunia?" asked Cotton the cat.

"When one is rich one is important, that's all," answered Petunia.

"Poor Petunia has lost her mind," said Canary the cow.

66

"I have lost nothing. I have *found* something," said Petunia. "I have found a treasure so big it has as many gold coins as there are stars in the sky."

No one talked for a while. Such treasure demanded much thinking.

"Where is it?" asked Noisy the dog, at last.

"That is my secret," answered Petunia, and walked proudly away.

"What do people do who become so rich?" asked Piggy.

"Petunia, I should think, could buy us gifts," said Straw the horse. "For my part I would love a pair of wings to fly like Pegasus the horse."

"I need an alarm clock," said King the rooster. "It would help me sing at the right time every morning to wake up the farm."

"I wish nothing more than a peacock tail," said Turkey. "I would be so handsome. My hens would love it."

"What I want," said Rose the sheep, "is a fierce tiger head to put over mine so I would no longer be called meek and dull."

"Well," said Pig, "I loathe hearing '*He eats like a pig.*' If I had silver dishes, forks, and knives, I could show that pigs are gentlemen."

"They say that I am a very pretty cow," said Canary. "Petunia could give me a large mirror so I could admire myself."

"All I want," said Goat, "is a tightrope between the stable and barn roofs. I would dance on it to show that I am an acrobat."

"I am the one who keeps peace in this farm and thieves out of it," said Noisy. "I need a megaphone to make my bark thunder."

"Me," said Ida the hen, "I am happy just with my little chicks."

When night came they all retired to dream about their wishes.
Petunia also dreamed. She dreamed that frogs were scattering
her treasure at the bottom of the river. All night, in her sleep,
she fought and chased the frogs. At dawn she was weary, and
she looked like a porcupine with the straw from her litter cling-
ing to her feathers.

When she came out of her coop, the barnyard animals were
waiting to greet their rich friend.

"Good morning, Petunia dear. Good morning and how do you
do?"

"Did you sleep well, Petunia?" asked Pig. "How were your
dreams?"

"You are a little tired under the eyes," said Ida. "It must be
the worries of wealth."

"Petunia," said Canary, "please take care of yourself. I will be
glad to wait for the mirror I want from you."

"And don't worry too much about my megaphone," said Noisy.

"Or about the alarm clock I need," said King.

"I can also wait for my silverware," said Pig.

"And I for my peacock tail," said Turkey.

More animals came to greet Petunia.

"Dearest Petunia," said Donkey, "give me a horse's tail, please. I hate my tail. It makes me look like a cow. But no hurry."

"Darling Petunia," said Clover the cow, "I want a horse's tail, too, and also a mane. I so wish to look like a handsome horse."

"For me it will be a balloon," said Piggy. "But take your time."

Then Coquet, Lily, and Nina, the hens, asked for ribbons, necklaces, and rings. "We are ladies and we must look like ladies. But we can also wait."

Poor rich Petunia. After the frogs made her night so troublesome, now came her friends to make her day difficult!

"My friends," said Petunia, nodding her head like a tired queen, "I hardly know how to express my gratitude. Your patience and your kindness warm my heart." And she walked off with majesty to rest in the shade of an apple tree.

"Oh," she thought, "how much wisdom one needs to bear the worry of riches—riches that are at the bottom of a river."

That night in her dream, Petunia opened the treasure chest
and saw a crocodile curled up inside. "Well, if it isn't Petunia,"
said the crocodile. "Don't look for your treasure, Petunia. *I ate it*.
But don't worry, you will see it presently, for I will eat you too."
The crocodile opened his mouth wide, so wide Petunia could see
the treasure shine inside him, and then . . . she woke up in time.

76

In the barnyard the animals again waited for her respectfully.

"Dearest Petunia," said Straw, "we all admire how bravely you endure the cares of wealth."

"Petunia," said Ida, "you look more tired than yesterday. Are you sick?"

"Petunia," said Canary, "if your treasure worries you, waiting for my mirror worries me too. How long shall I have to wait?"

"And my silver dinnerware?" asked Pig. "When shall I receive it?"

"Petunia," said King, "if you do not give me my alarm clock, I will stop singing in the morning."

"And what about my tiger head," growled Sheep.

"And my peacock tail?" asked Turkey.

"Shame on you," scolded Cotton the cat. "You spoiled, greedy animals! Can't you leave Petunia in peace?"

"Yes," said Ida, "she has so much on her mind that is important."

"Mind! Mind your own affairs," groaned Pig. "I know what I need!"

"Stop your nonsense or I'll bite you," snapped Noisy at Pig. "As for myself I no longer want a megaphone. I can shout loud enough."

"I want my mirror!" bellowed Canary.

"I'll kick you if you don't stop asking," threatened Straw. "I'll do without my wings. You can do without your mirror."

"You wouldn't threaten us if I had my tiger head!" cried Sheep.

Whereupon Goat horned Straw who kicked Pig who bit Noisy
who bit Canary who bit Ida who bit Sheep who bit Cotton who

82

scratched Goat. All the animals bit or scratched and clawed each other. The war was on in the Pumpkins' barnyard.

Full of woe, Petunia flew off to find peace on the riverbank. "I wish a real crocodile *had* eaten my treasure," she thought. "I was so silly to believe it would make me important and happy. It only brought me worries, and war among my friends."

Still, Petunia dove into the river to look at her treasure. Oh, what a surprise! The trunk was on its side, wide open. A frog sat on its lid; a rock lay in its bottom. There was no treasure.

"Stop worrying and be happy again, Petunia," said the frog. "Your treasure chest was an old trunk that was thrown here with a stone in it to weigh it down. When the river overflowed during the last rain, the trunk fell on its side and the lid opened."

"What a relief," sighed Petunia. "Now we can all be a friendly family again." Humming cheerfully, she walked back to the farm.

The barnyard war stopped when she entered with dancing steps.

"What's up now?" asked Cotton. "Did you find another treasure?"

"I found I have no treasure at all," said Petunia, "and that is the best treasure, for now we can all be happy together again."

How amazed the animals were! Their fighting now seemed so silly. They all laughed—the greedy ones louder than the others.

"At last there will be no more selfish begging," said Cotton.

"It is so nice Petunia can be one of us again," said Ida.

And all the barnyard joined Petunia in lively dancing and singing. Even the frog came to the party. It was a happy day.

PETUNIA'S

CHRISTMAS

The new snow was soft like a kitten's fur. Petunia liked it that way, and she went out for a walk to feel it with her feet. She saw that the deer, the rabbit, the squirrel, were also out in the snow. They were hunting for food.

Petunia went up the hill, through the woods, down the valley,
where she slipped into a tailspin on the frozen stream.

"The country looks all new when it's like this," thought
Petunia. "It's lovely like the farmhouse when it's freshly
painted." But the walk made her hungry, and she searched for
food through the snow.

When she reached Windy Farm, on the other side of the
stream, Petunia was stopped by a call: "Yohoo . . . pssttt . . .
yohoooo . . ."

Who could be calling her? Petunia was very curious. She ran
over to see.

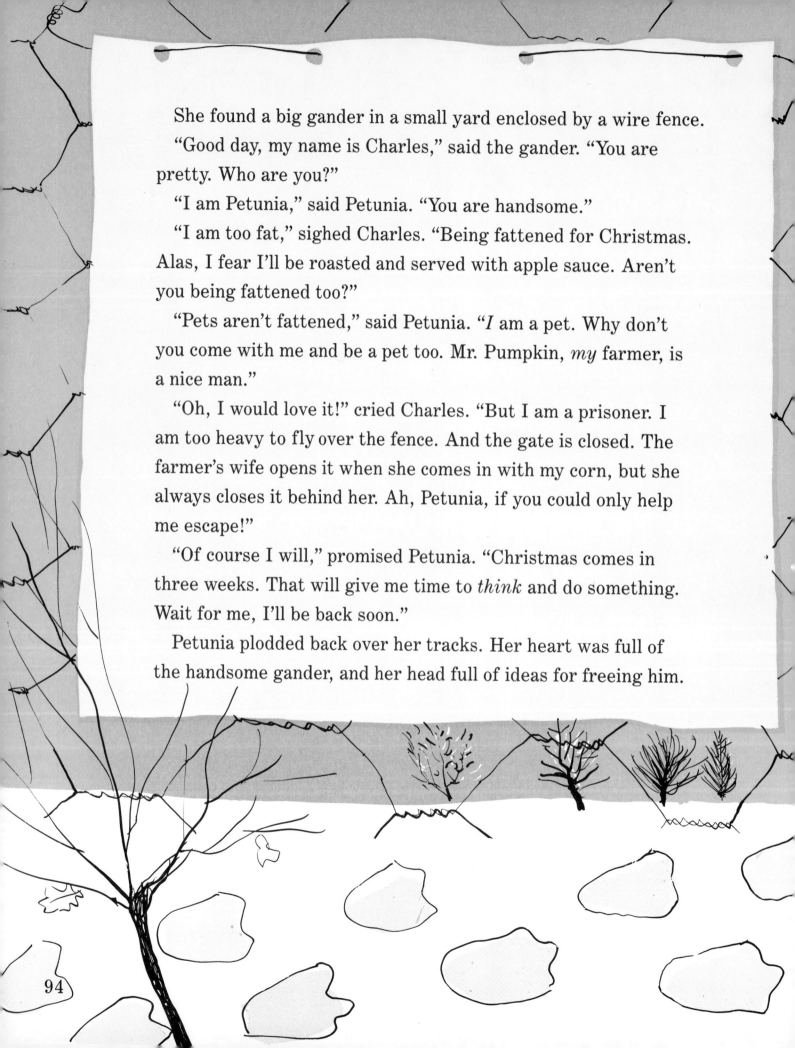

She found a big gander in a small yard enclosed by a wire fence.

"Good day, my name is Charles," said the gander. "You are pretty. Who are you?"

"I am Petunia," said Petunia. "You are handsome."

"I am too fat," sighed Charles. "Being fattened for Christmas. Alas, I fear I'll be roasted and served with apple sauce. Aren't you being fattened too?"

"Pets aren't fattened," said Petunia. "*I* am a pet. Why don't you come with me and be a pet too. Mr. Pumpkin, *my* farmer, is a nice man."

"Oh, I would love it!" cried Charles. "But I am a prisoner. I am too heavy to fly over the fence. And the gate is closed. The farmer's wife opens it when she comes in with my corn, but she always closes it behind her. Ah, Petunia, if you could only help me escape!"

"Of course I will," promised Petunia. "Christmas comes in three weeks. That will give me time to *think* and do something. Wait for me, I'll be back soon."

Petunia plodded back over her tracks. Her heart was full of the handsome gander, and her head full of ideas for freeing him.

95

Petunia lost no time when she arrived at her farm. She brought the cold-water paint from the toolshop and painted herself into a fairy-tale monster. She looked so fierce that she was afraid to look at herself in the mirror.

Then she returned to Windy Farm, all painted up. The fox came to meet her on the way, for he had smelled goose flesh; but he ran off in fright at the sight of her.

Up at Windy Farm, Petunia waited behind the barn for the
farmer's wife to come out with the corn for Charles. She waited
and waited until her feet were cold; and for goose feet, that's
very, very cold. But the farmer's wife came at last, and as soon
as she had unlocked the gate . . .

Petunia shot out from behind the barn making terrific war-honks.

Honk! Honk! Honk!

"Help! Help! A flying dragon!" shrieked the farmer's wife. She fled to the house. So there . . . the gate was open!

Charles came out. He walked off with Petunia over the hill—free.

But that was not all. The farmer heard his wife's cries and got
his two-barrel gun and went to shoot the flying dragon. He found
the tracks in the snow—Charles' big tracks, and Petunia's. "It's
a goose-footed flying dragon," he muttered. "And it stole my fine
gander." So with his gun cocked, he followed the tracks over the
hill, and through the woods, and right into Mr. Pumpkin's farm.

"Well, neighbor," said Mr. Pumpkin, "what do you want to shoot on my farm with your big gun?"

"The flying dragon that stole my fine gander," said the hunter. "Look! Its tracks lead to your barn . . ."

At that moment, Petunia came out of the barn, honking her loudest honks. But the hunter did not run like his wife, for he had a gun. He aimed it.

"Don't shoot! It's Petunia!" cried Mr. Pumpkin. "I know her voice . . ."

"Petunia? What's that?" asked the hunter, resting his gun.

"She's our pet goose! Why, neighbor, she almost scared me, too!"

101

While Mr. Pumpkin admired Petunia's war paint, the hunter went into the barn, where he found Charles hidden in a pile of hay.

"You will escape no more," said the hunter as he led Charles away.

"A twenty-pound goose at seventy-five cents a pound, that's more than I can afford to lose."

Poor Petunia,
how she cried!

She loved Charles so.

But then she thought of the
farmer's words: "Twenty pounds
at seventy-five cents."

"Twenty times seventy-five
cents. That's a lot
of money. If I had it,
I could buy Charles's
freedom.

"I am going to earn it."

So Petunia began the easy way—she thought.

But people were too busy to stop and read her sign. They went
on about their business, and few pennies dropped into Petunia's
cup. She would never earn Charles's freedom that way. Time was
too short.

So she went to the woods to gather a load of pine twigs, which
she brought to the barn.

The barn smelled nice with the pine scent. Petunia sat among
the twigs, and she tied them into beautiful Christmas wreaths
with red ribbons.

When she trotted out of town with the wreaths piled all over
her, Petunia was the gayest Christmas goose you ever saw.

People liked her so much that they flocked around her like
children around a window full of toys.

Everyone wanted Petunia's wreaths. Some even asked
whether they could buy her, too. She soon went home with her
cup full of coins.

Petunia counted the coins three times on the barn floor, but there were not enough. Not enough to buy all of Charles's twenty pounds. Poor Charles. She must make more wreaths to sell.

Petunia made more wreaths; she made paper angels; she made stars; paper Christmas trees, and other Christmas things. And she went to town again to sell them. At last she had enough money. Even enough to buy a few extra pounds—just in case.

But was it not too late now? Christmas was so near. Petunia
almost flew to Windy Farm with a bag full of coins.

Oh, joy! Charles was still there, in his yard.

The farmer and his wife opened their eyes big as Christmas
tree balls when Petunia offered the bag of coins in exchange for
Charles's freedom.

They were good-hearted. The farmer's wife wiped her eyes
with the corner of her apron when she thought of Petunia's
devotion. They would not take the bag of coins.

"Charles is free," the farmer said. "Keep the coins for a happy
Christmas."

Charles and Petunia thanked the good farmer and his wife,
and they went out together over the hill.

Petunia and Charles were married on Christmas day. The barnyard had never seen so much dancing, singing, and feasting.

It was a very, very merry Christmas.

And Petunia and Charles were happy ever after.

PETUNIA
TAKES A TRIP

Every day the shiny silver plane flew over the little farm in the valley.

And every day Petunia, and Charley the gander,

and their goslings, watched . . .

until it vanished beyond the distant hills.

"Where does it come from?" asked the goslings. "Where does it go?"

"Ah, it comes from far away," said Petunia. "And it goes where the sky goes, far, far away. It must be nice, far away."

One day, Petunia said: "*Watch me!* I am going to fly up to the sky, like the plane, and see how big the world is beyond the hills. I will come back presently to tell you what I saw."

Petunia flapped her wings so furiously that the grasses bent their heads. But she rose no higher than the rabbit jumps, and then she fell on her head . . . *plump!*

"I know what's wrong with you," said Charley the gander. "You are almost as fat as I am. Go and climb on the scale and see."

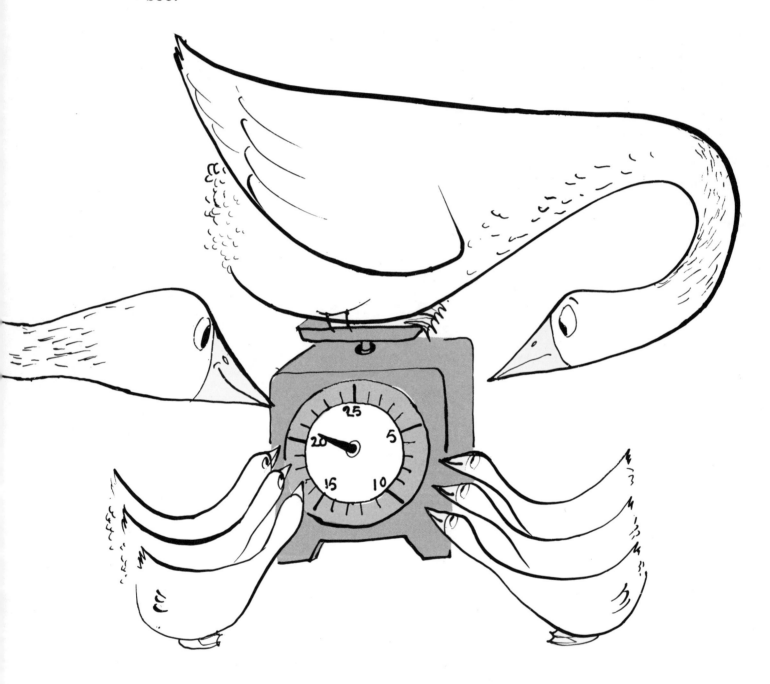

Petunia did see! "Twenty pounds!" she cried.
"Twenty pounds! Hoo . . . oo," cried the goslings.
"A twenty-pound goose can't fly to the sky," said Charley.

"Well," said Petunia, "I know what I'll do—
C-A-L-I-S-TH-E-N-I-C-S!
"Lots of CALISTHENICS; until I am light enough to fly."
And she did calisthenics in the middle of the farmyard, every
morning and every afternoon. Like this . . .

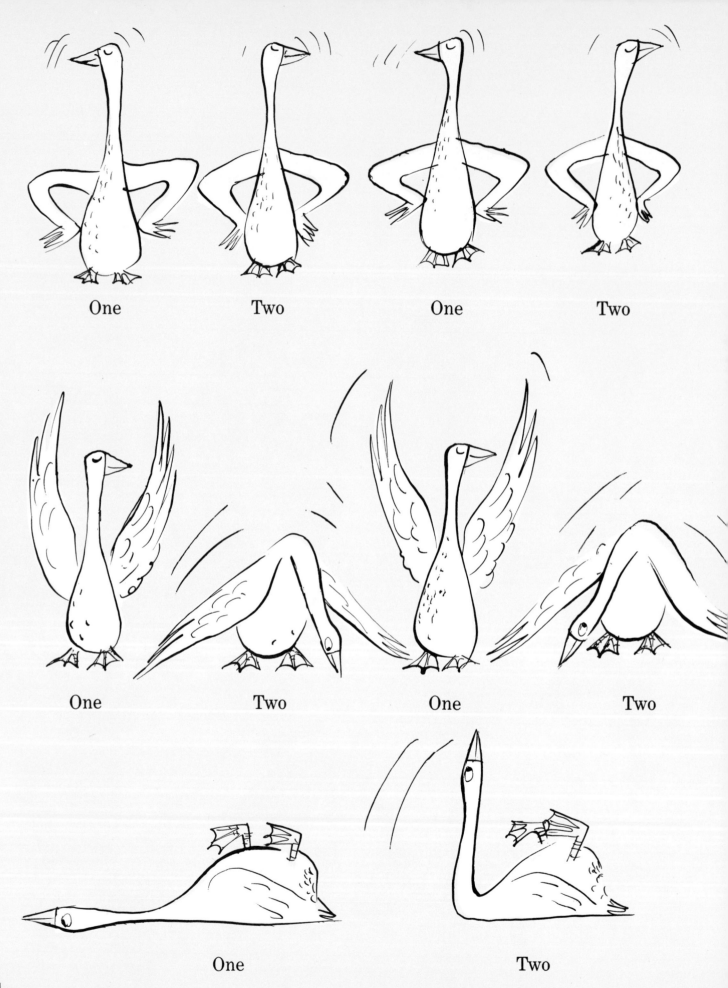

One   Two   One   Two

One   Two   One   Two

One   Two

One

Two

One

Two

One

Two

Before long Petunia was as slender as the guinea hen. She was strong, too—so strong that she decided the time had come to try her wings again.

She went to the meadow, and after a short run—*zoom!*—she climbed up on her great white wings.

It worked!

She climbed higher and higher, over the heads of her cheering friends . . .

. . . higher and higher over the little farm . . . and over the hills . . .
higher and higher until the earth below was like a soft green
rug, and tiny red and white dots were all she could see of the
farm buildings. She made sharp turns, right and left; she glided
like the eagle. She had the sky all to herself. It was wonderful.

But in her joy Petunia did not see the dark clouds coming toward her. Before she could flee, a high wind blew them all around her, lightning blinded her, and she was carried away by an angry storm. Blown about the black clouds like a leaf, she could not tell which way was up and which was down.

When at last the sky cleared, Petunia saw, far below, a very strange sight. The whole earth was laid with rows of houses set close together like stones in a wall. The rows opened only to let through two rivers full of busy boats.

"Oh, what an adventure," said Petunia, above the big city.
"Where am I? What am I going to do?" She was so tired she
simply let herself down and alighted at a street crossing.

Petunia was quite frightened at first. So many noises, so many people, so many cars—and so many windows above! Happily, as the policeman blew his whistle to stop the traffic, a taxi driver cried:

"Petunia! . . . It's Petunia!"

"A thousand whistles," said the policeman. "So it is."

The crowd pressed around Petunia to pet her, but the policeman and the taxi driver saw that she was hungry and tired and
they whisked her away in the taxicab to the cafeteria around the
corner.

Within the illustration:

HAM & CHEESE 3 Decker 35¢

ITALIAN STYLE SPAGHETTI

WHEAT CAKES 20¢ Special Today

COUNTRY SAUSAGES DELICIOUS 2 Fried Eggs 40¢

HAMBURGER spaghetti 30

COFFEE 10¢
MILK 10¢
CHOCOLATE 10¢

While Petunia ate a triple-decker sandwich, the policeman and the taxi driver told her about their city, how beautiful and big it was.

"Why," said the policeman, "most houses are bigger than your farmhouse, barns, and silo put together."

"And wait," said the taxi driver. "You
wouldn't believe it, even our animals are
bigger." And they drove Petunia to a place
where trees and grass grew and animals
were kept. Indeed, city animals were not
at all like those on the farm. Some were so
tall—as tall as maypoles.

And Petunia felt smaller looking up at
them . . .

smaller . . .   and smaller . . .

136

"Wait," said the policeman. "You have not seen the biggest one." And they took Petunia to a house where an animal as large as a barn stood quietly munching peanuts.

He was so big Petunia felt still smaller.

"Wait," said the taxi driver. "That's nothing. You haven't seen
the boats in the city." And they drove Petunia to the riverside,
where boats as big as hills were tied with ropes as big as trees.
They were so big, Petunia felt still smaller.

138

"Wait," said the policeman. "You haven't seen the deepest
street in the city." And they drove Petunia to a street as deep as
a crevice in the mountain.

It was so deep, Petunia, at the bottom, felt still smaller.

139

"Wait," said the taxi driver. "You haven't seen the tallest house in the city." And they drove Petunia to a place where there was a house so tall that its roof was hidden in the clouds. So tall, Petunia felt still smaller. (She is the smaller dot in the right corner. The larger dots are the policeman, the taxi driver, and the taxicab.)

"Wait," said the policeman. "I will show you the house in which my wife and I live." And they drove Petunia to a house so big it would have held *all* the farmhouses in Petunia's village with their barns and their silos.

Petunia now felt so small she feared she was in danger of disappearing altogether. You cannot see her here. She is so small.

And she was worried to think she had shrunk so. She *must* return to her farm or there would be no more Petunia. But the policeman and Petunia thanked the taxi driver for the beautiful ride and they went up to the policeman's apartment.

In the apartment Petunia saw a sparrow picking crumbs on the window sill and she felt at once a little bigger again.

"How can you live in the big city?" she asked him. "You are so small! You would be happier on a farm."

"I don't like farms," said the sparrow. "There aren't enough windows for crumbs. I manage very well here, thank you."

"You are so tiny anyway, it makes little difference, I suppose."

"Why don't you go back to your farm?" asked the sparrow.

"It's too far for me to fly. The storm blew me here, but it won't blow me back to my farm."

"Sorry," said the busy sparrow, "but I see some crumbs over there. Good-bye, Petunia."

The policeman's wife was glad to see Petunia. She cooked a delicious dinner for her, and put her to sleep in a soft bed under the television. But she knew that Petunia was not happy.

"She misses her farm," she told her husband. "We must put her on the train tomorrow."

The next day the policeman and his wife took Petunia to a railroad station so big it would have enclosed a mountain. They kissed Petunia and Petunia waved to them when the train started off.

"Come and visit me in the country!" she cried to her kind friends.

143

From her seat by the train window, Petunia watched the green fields, the *small* houses, the *small* streams, as they glided by, and she felt more and more like a real-size goose again. She was happy.

"It's good to go home," she said to herself.

In the *small* station of her village, she was greeted by
Charley, the goslings, and all her normal-size farmyard friends.
And that night she slept happily in her normal-size house.

Many a time afterward she told her children about the beautiful, big, *big* world one could see beyond the hills.

ROGER DUVOISIN

is widely recognized as one of the foremost author-illustrators of children's books of this century. He was born in Geneva in 1904 and worked as an artist in Switzerland and France before coming to this country in the early 1930s to design silks for an American textile firm. His first book, *A Little Boy Is Drawing*, which he made as a gift to his young son, was published in 1932. In the years since then, until his death in 1980, he illustrated forty books that he had written, and more than a hundred books by other authors, among them *The Happy Lion* and its sequels, written by Louise Fatio, his wife. Throughout his career he won many awards, including the Caldecott Medal in 1947 for *White Snow, Bright Snow* by Alvin Tresselt, and a Caldecott Honor in 1966 for *Hide and Seek*, also by Tresselt. He is perhaps best remembered now for his gently humorous picture books featuring such distinctive animal characters as Veronica, the conspicuous hippopotamus, and, most notably, Petunia, the silly goose.